What If?

by Robert Pierce

MERRIGOLD PRESS • NEW YORK

©1969 Merrigold Press, Racine, Wisconsin 53402. All rights reserved.
Printed in the U.S.A. No part of this book may be reproduced or copied
in any form without written permission from the publisher.
All trademarks are the property of Merrigold Press. Library of Congress
Catalog Card Number: 75-81961 ISBN: 0-307-90951-4   MCMXCI

WHAT IF an elephant
Climbed your stairs?

What if your closet
Was full of bears?

What if a kangaroo
Came to cook?

And a tiger read you
A story book?

What if a seal
And a tall giraffe
Did magic tricks
To make you laugh?

If all this happened
What would you do?
The answer is easy—

START A ZOO!

WHAT IF a walrus
Played trombone?

RAZZAZZA
MAZZAZZ

BORNKITY
BORNK

And a hippo hammered
A xylophone?

What if an ostrich
All in a dither,

LA DI DA

TWING
TWANG

Danced to the tune
Of a zebra's zither?

What if some yaks
And a unicorn
Played drums and sax
And a big bass horn?

What could you do
With the noise they made?
What do you think?

HAVE A PARADE!

RAT-A-
TAT TAT   HONK   TWING
TWANG   RAZZAZZA
MAZZAZZ

WHAT IF birthdays
Came twice a week?

MAY 15

MAY 18

And behind your house
Was a lemonade creek?

What if rocks
Were made of cheese?

And baseballs grew
On baseball trees?

What if cookies fell
And hit your nose?

And ice cream oozed
From the garden hose?

What if your friends
Were jolly and hearty?
What would you do?

HAVE A PARTY!

WHAT IF a green
And purple snake—

Gobbled up all
Of the birthday cake?

What if your bathtub
Was full of frogs?

What if it <u>really</u> rained
Cats and dogs?

What if a crocodile
Big as an ox—

Hid in the hallway
And ate your socks?

Or a lion was having
A masquerade ball—
What would you do?

INVITE THEM ALL!